The Five Senses of Love

Janet Parsons • Claire Richards

Sandy Creek
NEW YORK

For Carmel, Marjorie and Kevin Flew, with love, grace and gratitude.
My first and greatest teachers for living a life of love in action. *Janet Parsons*

For Auntie Denise for teaching me craft, for Auntie Rosie for coming to my art shows
and Auntie Margie for sending pencils and encouragement. *Claire Richards*

Sandy Creek
NEW YORK

An Imprint of Sterling Publishing
387 Park Avenue South
New York, NY 10016

Text © 2010 by Janet Parsons
Illustrations © 2010 by Claire Richards

This 2012 custom edition is published exclusively for Sandy Creek by Potoroo Publishing – Melbourne, Australia

Text design, Carol Nicholls

ISBN 978-1-4351-4514-6

Manufactured in Nansha CHINA
Lot #:
2 4 6 8 10 9 7 5 3 1
09/12

The very best news about love
is that it is absolutely everywhere, all the time,
and I can find it with any of my five senses.

I can see love in Mom's eyes
when she tells me the story of
the night I was born.

I can see love at the airport
when I go to pick up my Dad,

...or when Grandpa comes to watch my concert.

That's when I see love.

I can hear love when my brother
pushes me on my swing and
the wind whistles past my ears.

I can hear love when a baby laughs,

...and when I am running in a race and hear the crowd calling my name.

That's when I hear love.

I can smell love in the kitchen
when my dinner is being cooked.

I can smell love when I blow out
my birthday candles and make a wish.

Love is in the air when my Grandma gives me her biggest cuddle, in a cloud of perfume.

That's when I smell love.

I can taste love when I toast a marshmallow.

I can taste love
in the yummy food
packed in my lunchbox,

...and especially when I eat ice cream with my friends.

That's when I taste love.

I can feel love when
I paint with my fingers.

I can feel love when
I am pushing the baby's stroller,

...and when I am wrapped in a warm, safe bear hug.

That's when I feel love.

Even when I am all alone,
I can still feel love when I hold my
own hand and squeeze it three times
and say to myself, "I LOVE YOU!"